YAWN

STRETCH

STRETCH

For **GARY NORTHFIELD**
Ace Dinosaur Comics Artist

Edited by Pauliina Malinen
Cover designed by Strawberrie Donnelly
Designed by Rebecca Essilfie

First published in 2015 by Scholastic Children's Books
This edition published in 2017
Euston House, 24 Eversholt Street, London NW1 1DB
a division of Scholastic Ltd
www.scholastic.co.uk

London - New York - Toronto - Sydney - Auckland
Mexico City - New Delhi - Hong Kong

DINOSAUR POLICE

BY

SARAH
McIntyre

SCHOLASTIC

Dinoville police station was having a perfectly quiet morning – until the phone rang…

"RED ALERT!" hollered Sergeant Stig O'Saurus. "There's a rampaging T-Rex at the pizza factory!"

Sergeant Stig O'Saurus and Inspector Sarah Tops were on their way, faster than you can say "WOO WOO".

Officer Brachio joined in, even though he was too big to fit in the car.

The pizza factory was a **mess**.
Inspector Sarah sighed,
"I should have guessed...
it's Trevor the **T-Rex!**"

The manager was sobbing, "The mayor ordered these pizzas for tomorrow's town fair. Everything is ruined!"

"We'll catch this T-Rex," promised Sergeant Stig.

Trevor had eaten
SO MUCH PIZZA
that he fell asleep.

Inspector Sarah said,
"Right, let's take him
to the station."

Sergeant Stig switched on his megaphone.

ZZZZzz
SNORTLE
SNORE...

WAKE UP
TREVOR!

But what was this...?
Trevor's arms were so tiny that they slipped through the handcuffs!

AWRR!

bellowed Trevor as he made a run for it.

But did Trevor listen?
"RAWRRR!" he roared, as he crashed
and stomped through the building site,
with the air squad hot on his heels.

What a fiasco!
Could ANYONE stop that T-Rex?

It wasn't the air squad that caught Trevor.
It wasn't the police.

It was the CEMENT!

Trevor was completely STUCK. He let out a whine of panic.

"TREVOR," said Inspector Sarah, "we'll get you out, but only if you promise not to run away."

"RAWRRRR" agreed Trevor.

Back at the station, the dinosaur police hosed off the rest of the cement.

Trevor blushed like a tomato. **"I'M SORRY,"** he said to the manager of the pizza factory.

"I'm glad you said sorry," said the manager. "But how are we going to make enough pizzas for tomorrow's fair?"

"I WILL HELP!" offered Trevor.

The dinosaurs prepared pizzas all through the night.

Trevor tried to help, but he was feeling clumsy and bloated and made more mess than pizzas.

The mayor arrived the next morning. "Thank you for the pizzas!" she said. "But why is there a gloomy T-Rex hiding in the corner?"

The manager told her the whole story.

"Hmm," said the mayor. "I have an idea..."

"**WHEE!!**" shouted the baby dinosaurs. **BOING! BOING!** Nothing bounces as well as a big bloated T-Rex.

Everyone tucked into the yummy pizzas – everyone except Trevor, who still felt mighty full. Trevor was so happy he let out a little BURP, and all the baby dinosaurs joined in!

BAWRPP
BUUURP
RAAARP
FRIP
MORNING BREATH? THAT'S NOT FRESH!!
I THINK I JUST SET A WORLD BURP RECORD!
THIS BURP'S GOING TO GO DOWN IN HISTORY!
KIDS WILL STUDY IT IN SCHOOLS.